Forever
Friends

Fulton Books, Inc.
Meadville, PA

Published by Fulton Books 2021

ISBN 978-1-63710-990-8 (paperback)
ISBN 978-1-63710-991-5 (digital)

Printed in the United States of America

Forever Friends

CHRIS COKLEY

Illustrated by: Brayden Heiges

The sun was bright.
It was a warm day,
when Aubree's parents
took her to the park to play.

Aubree loved the park,
the grass so green, the trees so tall,
and at the heart of the park
was a fountain she loved most of all!

Just past the fountain
there were playgrounds for fun.
The park was full of people
enjoying the summer sun.

There were children on the swings
and sliding down the slide.
Aubree was feeling very shy
and stayed by her father's side.

"Don't you want to play?" asked her dad.
"You can make friends with anyone here."
Aubree shrugged her shoulders
and deep inside she felt a little fear.

Aubree wasn't sure if she could have fun.
The playground was full of kids she didn't know.
She began to worry that the day was done;
all she could think was "I want to go."

Her father smiled warmly and said,
"Remember that everyone is a possible friend."
Aubree smiled back and nodded her head.
"And the best friendships never end."

Aubree looked across the playground,
and there she saw Angela playing all alone.

She was talking into a stick she found;
she was pretending it was a phone.

Aubree was taught how to make friends.

First, introduce yourself. "Hi, I'm Aubree."

Next, you simply ask very nicely,

"Would you like to play with me?"

Angela did not have to think twice.

She said, "Yes! Angela is my name!"

Angela smiled, and they both laughed,

and they went off to play a game.

Angela and Aubree were nothing alike.

They looked as different as night and day.

But that made no difference to them;
they were happy and just wanted to play.

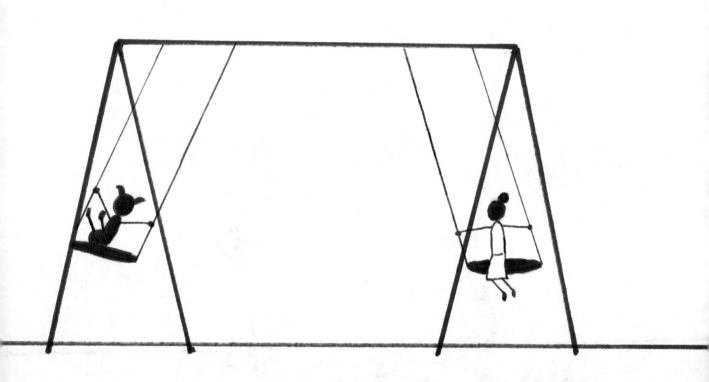

Never judge possible friends by their looks
and making friends can be as easy as pie.
When it comes to being a good friend,
all you ever have to do is try.

Try to be forgiving.

Try to share what's on your mind.

Try to be patient.

Above everything else, try to be kind.

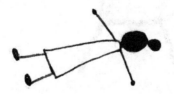

Try to be nice.
Always try to share.
Try to listen carefully.
Always try to be fair

Aubree and Angela played all day.
And when Aubree's father called her name,
she didn't want to leave her newfound friend,
and she shouted back, "Just one more game?"

Aubree's father laughed and nodded.
"You can stay and play one more!"
Aubree and Angela didn't know it then,
but they had a lifetime of friendship in store.

About the Author

Chris Cokley is a twenty-five year old young author who grew up on the East side of Savannah, Georgia, where he was always able to make a friend no matter the color. Chris wants to grasp the attention of young readers and teach them that friendship is based on kindness and the love in your heart and not judged by the color of one's skin.